WOULD RATHER?

EWW! YUCK! GROSS!

This way to crazy, ridiculous
and downright hilarious
'Would You Rathers?!'

WARNING!
These are Eww! These are Yuck! These
are Gross! And they are really funny!
Laughter awaits!

RatherFunnyPress.com

Books By
RATHER FUNNY PRESS

Would You Rather? For 6 Year Old Kids!
Would You Rather? For 7 Year Old Kids!
Would You Rather? For 8 Year Old Kids!
Would You Rather? For 9 Year Old Kids!
Would You Rather? For 10 Year Old Kids!
Would You Rather? For 11 Year Old Kids!
Would You Rather? For 12 Year Old Kids!
Would You Rather? For Teens!
Would You Rather? Eww! Yuck! Gross!

To see all the latest books by
Rather Funny Press just go to
RatherFunnyPress.com

YOUR
FREE SURPRISE GIFT!

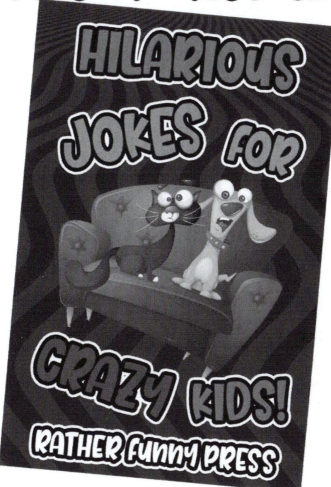

Details on the last page of this book!
A brand new free joke book
just for you.
Check it out! Laughter awaits!

HOW TO PLAY

This easy to play game is a ton of fun!
Have 2 or more players.
The first reader will choose a 'Would You Rather?'
from the book and read it aloud.
The other player(s) then choose which scenario
they would prefer and why.
You can't say 'neither' or 'none'.
You must choose one and explain why.
Then the book is passed to the next person
and the game continues!

The main rule is have fun, laugh and enjoy
spending time with your friends and family.
Let the fun begin!

ATTENTION!

All the scenarios and choices in this book are
fictional and meant to be about using your
imagination, having a ton of fun and enjoying this
game with your friends and family.
Obviously, DO NOT ATTEMPT any of these
scenarios in real life.

WOULD YOU RATHER...

PICK YOUR TEACHER'S NOSE

OR

CLIP THEIR TOENAILS?

SWIM IN A RIVER OF
HIPPOPOTAMUS WEE

OR

CANNONBALL INTO A
POOL OF SNOT?

WOULD YOU RATHER...

ALWAYS HAVE REALLY BAD
GARLIC BREATH

OR

HAVE DISGUSTING ONION
SCENTED BODY ODOR?

FART OUT OF BOTH
EARS AT ONCE

OR

BE ABLE TO CONTROL WHICH
EAR YOU FARTED OUT OF?

WOULD YOU RATHER...

CLEAN THE TOILET LID WITH
YOUR TONGUE

OR

DRINK A CUP OF
TOILET WATER?

STEP ON A POOP WHILE
RUNNING BAREFOOT
AT THE BEACH

OR

HAVE A POOP FLOAT BY WHILE
RELAXING IN THE HOT TUB?

WOULD YOU RATHER...

EAT A BOWL OF
WRIGGLING WORMS

OR

A BOWL OF DEAD
COCKROACHES?

SLEEP IN A CAT'S USED
LITTER TRAY FOR A NIGHT

OR

ONLY BE ABLE TO EAT PEAS FOR
THE REST OF YOUR LIFE?

WOULD YOU RATHER...

EAT A SNAIL ALIVE

OR

DO A FART IN A HAT AND
THEN WEAR IT?

ALWAYS STINK AND
NOT KNOW IT

OR

EVERYONE ELSE STINKS AND
THEY DON'T KNOW IT?

WOULD YOU RATHER...

LICK THE ARMPIT OF A SWEATY HIKER

OR

LICK THE EARWAX OF AN OLD MAN?

HAVE A PET WORM THAT LIVED IN YOUR NOSE

OR

A PET FLY THAT LIVED IN YOUR EAR?

WOULD YOU RATHER...

HAVE YOUR FART SMELL LIKE ROAST CHICKEN

OR

STRONG COFFEE?

ONLY BE ABLE TO BATHE ONCE A YEAR

OR

ONLY BE ABLE TO WASH YOUR CLOTHES ONCE A YEAR?

WOULD YOU RATHER...

SLEEP IN YOUR PARENTS' BED EVERY NIGHT

OR

CRY UNCONTROLLABLY EVERY TIME SOMEONE TELLS YOU A JOKE?

PUT A LIVE CRAB DOWN YOUR UNDERPANTS

OR

DRINK A FULL CUP OF ROTTEN CRAB JUICE THROUGH YOUR NOSE?

WOULD YOU RATHER...

HAVE YOUR FARTS SOUND LIKE A CAR HORN

OR

A LION ROARING?

STEP IN DOG POOP EVERY TIME YOU LEAVE THE HOUSE

OR

HAVE A BIRD POOP ON YOU EVERY TIME YOU LEAVE THE HOUSE?

WOULD YOU RATHER...

SIT IN A ROOM FULL OF COCKROACHES

OR

A ROOM FULL OF FLYING, SCREECHING BIRDS?

DRINK EEL JUICE WITH YOUR BREAKFAST

OR

WATCH YOUR FAMILY HAVE A FART COMPETITION IN FRONT OF YOUR TEACHER?

WOULD YOU RATHER...

HAVE TO WEAR SECOND HAND UNDERWEAR

OR

USE A SECOND HAND TOOTHBRUSH?

HAVE THE BIGGEST BUTT IN THE HISTORY OF HUMANITY

OR

NO BUTT AT ALL?

WOULD YOU RATHER...

EAT A BOWL OF
DEAD INSECTS

OR

A PIECE OF RAW MEAT?

GARGLE MOUTHWASH THAT HAS
ALREADY BEEN GARGLED BY
YOUR GRANDMA

OR

FLOSS YOUR TEETH WITH FLOSS
THAT HAS ALREADY BEEN USED
BY YOUR DAD?

WOULD YOU RATHER...

THAT EVERY TIME YOU EAT A BANANA IT TURNS INTO A MASSIVE CENTIPEDE

OR

A GIANT WORM?

GET A FREE HELICOPTER RIDE BUT THE PILOT IS REALLY ANNOYING

OR

GET A FREE HELICOPTER RIDE BUT THE PILOT DOES ONE SUPER STINKY FART A MINUTE?

WOULD YOU RATHER...

EAT LIVE MAGGOTS

OR

POOP OUT LIVE MAGGOTS?

HAVE 1,000 COCKROACHES
IN YOUR BEDROOM

OR

HAVE A BATH WITH 1,000
WRIGGLING WORMS?

WOULD YOU RATHER...

LICK A STRANGER'S EYE
FOR 10 SECONDS

OR

LICK A STRANGER'S SCAB
FOR 2 SECONDS?

DO REALLY LOUD FARTS THAT
DIDN'T SMELL AT ALL

OR

SILENT FARTS THAT SMELT
REALLY BAD?

WOULD YOU RATHER...

PLAY IN A MUD PIT FILLED
WITH WORMS AND
3 MYSTERIOUS POOPS

OR

PLAY IN A BATH OF BAKED
BEANS AND BOOGERS?

SWIM IN A POOL OF
ROTTING FISH

OR

SIT IN A BATH OF SOUR
MILK?

WOULD YOU RATHER...

LET A DUCK FART IN
YOUR FACE

OR

HAVE A MOUSE POOP ON YOUR
BREAKFAST CEREAL?

DRINK A WHOLE GLASS OF
LLAMA SPIT IN 5 SECONDS

OR

EAT AN OVERSIZED ICE CREAM
CONE FULL OF INSECTS?

WOULD YOU RATHER...

WEAR DIRTY UNDERWEAR

OR

WET UNDERWEAR?

LICK YOUR OWN TOILET SEAT

OR

EAT A MEAL OFF A BUSY RESTROOM TOILET SEAT?

WOULD YOU RATHER...

HAVE YOUR FART SOUND LIKE A CAT HISSING

OR

LIKE A VERY LOUD FOG HORN?

DO 4 SMELLY POOPS A DAY

OR

ONLY DO TWO GIANT POOPS THE SIZE OF A CAR EACH YEAR?

WOULD YOU RATHER...

HAVE NOSE HAIRS THAT WERE SO LONG THEY DRAGGED ON THE GROUND

OR

EYELASHES SO LONG NO-ONE CAN SEE YOUR FACE?

SIT IN A HOT TUB FULL OF SNAILS AND WORMS

OR

SWIM IN A POOL FULL OF ROTTEN FISH?

WOULD YOU RATHER...

HAVE A FARTING COMPETITION WITH YOUR DAD

OR

YOUR GRANDMA?

WEAR FISH SMELLING CLOTHES ON A FIRST DATE

OR

CLOTHES FIVE SIZES TOO BIG ON LIVE TV?

WOULD YOU RATHER...

DRINK THE BATHWATER OF A MAN WHO JUST HAD HIS FIRST BATH IN 12 YEARS

OR

EAT A ROTTEN LEG OF TURKEY?

HAVE A BATH IN 5 GALLONS OF HOT CHILLI SAUCE

OR

5 GALLONS OF VINEGAR?

WOULD YOU RATHER...

FALL DOWN A STAIRCASE MADE OF DEAD RATS

OR

MICROWAVE A DEAD RAT AND USE IT AS A HOT WATER BOTTLE?

PAINT A KITTEN ONLY USING THE GREENEST SNOT YOU CAN FIND

OR

LET A BABY KITTEN POOP ON YOUR TOAST?

WOULD YOU RATHER...

EAT YOUR TOENAIL CLIPPINGS

OR

EAT YOUR HAIR TRIMMINGS AFTER A HAIRCUT?

HAVE 5 PEOPLE FART NEAR YOU AT THE SAME TIME

OR

YOU HAVE TO DO A HUGE FART NEAR 5 PEOPLE YOU HAVE NEVER MET BEFORE?

WOULD YOU RATHER...

HAVE A PET SPIDER THAT LIVES IN YOUR HAIR

OR

A PET EARWIG THAT LIVES IN YOUR EAR?

CLEAN YOUR TOENAILS BY LICKING THEM WITH YOUR TONGUE

OR

CLEAN A SMELLY CAT BY LICKING IT WITH YOUR TONGUE?

WOULD YOU RATHER...

HAVE A WEIRD DISEASE WHERE SMELLY GREEN PUS COMES OUT OF YOUR NOSE

OR

OUT OF YOUR EARS?

HAVE AN EXTRA EYE ON YOUR FOREHEAD

OR

AN EXTRA EYE ON THE BACK OF YOUR HEAD?

WOULD YOU RATHER...

FART IN FRONT OF YOUR TEACHER

OR

FART LOUDLY IN A LIBRARY?

HAVE A JOB POPPING STRANGERS' PIMPLES

OR

PICKING THEIR NOSE AND LICKING THEIR BOOGERS?

WOULD YOU RATHER...

GET BITTEN BY A SPIDER

OR

STUNG BY 50 BEES?

HAVE EXTREMELY SWEATY
ARM PITS

OR

HAVE AN EXTREMELY
ITCHY BUTT?

WOULD YOU RATHER...

EAT A FROZEN SNOT POPSICLE

OR

BRUSH YOUR TEETH WITH
MASHED UP SLUGS?

HAVE A GIANT ONE INCH PIMPLE
ON THE END OF YOUR NOSE

OR

IN THE MIDDLE OF
YOUR FOREHEAD?

WOULD YOU RATHER...

GO DIVING WITH A SCUBA TANK FULL OF FARTS

OR

WEE ON AN ELECTRIC FENCE?

HAVE FINGERNAILS THAT SMELL LIKE STINKY BLUE CHEESE

OR

EAT A CHEESE PIZZA THAT SMELLS LIKE OLD, DIRTY SOCKS?

WOULD YOU RATHER...

EAT SOME WEEDS TOPPED WITH MELTED CHOCOLATE

OR

EAT A CHOCOLATE BAR COATED IN MUD?

LICK THE SNOT FROM THE RUNNY NOSE OF A HORSE

OR

EAT HALF A TEASPOON OF EARWAX FROM A KIND, ELDERLY GENTLEMAN?

WOULD YOU RATHER...

SMELL YOUR FRIEND'S BREATH

OR

SMELL YOUR FRIEND'S FART?

EAT MOULDY CHEESE

OR

A HALF EATEN CUPCAKE YOU FOUND IN THE BIN?

WOULD YOU RATHER...

EAT A COCKROACH PIZZA

OR

DRINK A BOOGER MILK SHAKE?

WEAR A WORM AS A RING

OR

WEAR A DEAD SKUNK
AS A HAT?

WOULD YOU RATHER...

EAT A CHUNK OF SKUNK HAIR

OR

DRINK A GLASS OF STINKY SWEAT?

WEAR A ROTTING STARFISH FOR A HAT

OR

SCUBA DIVE IN THE SEWERS?

WOULD YOU RATHER...

DRINK A USED DIAPER
SMOOTHIE

OR

DO A FRONT FLIP INTO A
SWIMMING POOL FULL OF
VOMIT?

GET CAUGHT SCRATCHING YOUR
BUTT FOR ONE MINUTE

OR

GET CAUGHT EATING
A BOOGER?

WOULD YOU RATHER...

CHALLENGE A FLATULENT LLAMA TO A FARTING COMPETITION

OR

EAT A GROSS SMELLING HOTDOG FROM A BIN?

DO A PEE INTO A BUCKET

OR

IN A SMALL CUP?

WOULD YOU RATHER...

HAVE A BITE OF A RAW ONION

OR

EAT A ROTTEN ORANGE?

SMELL LIKE A SKUNK
FOR A WEEK

OR

SMELL LIKE ROTTEN EGGS
FOR A MONTH?

WOULD YOU RATHER...

TAKE AN HOUR LONG BATH IN A TUB FULL OF OCTOPUSSES AND SNOT

OR

EAT A REGURGITATED CAT FUR-BALL?

EAT A LIVE WORM

OR

A DEAD CATERPILLAR?

WOULD YOU RATHER...

HAVE YOUR FART SMELL LIKE KFC

OR

APPLE PIE?

HAVE A LIVE COCKROACH IN YOUR MOUTH FOR ONE MINUTE

OR

A LIVE SPIDER IN YOUR MOUTH FOR 20 SECONDS?

WOULD YOU RATHER...

EAT A LOAF OF BREAD WITH MAGGOTS INSIDE

OR

PUT A MAGGOT IN YOUR NOSE?

SKYDIVE INTO A PILE OF DIRTY DIAPERS AND NOT BE INJURED

OR

BOUNCE ON A TRAMPOLINE AND BREAK YOUR ARM?

WOULD YOU RATHER...

BREATHE IN A BAG OF SMELLY FARTS

OR

EAT A BOWL OF ROTTEN RAW EGGS?

DO ONE REALLY BIG POOP ONCE A WEEK

OR

LOTS OF LITTLE POOPS FIVE TIMES A DAY?

WOULD YOU RATHER...

EAT A ROTTEN HAMBURGER

OR

LICK A SMELLY CHILD'S SHOE?

CLEAN YOUR BEST FRIEND'S EARS

OR

CLIP THEIR TOENAILS?

WOULD YOU RATHER...

LICK THE CLASSROOM FLOOR

OR

LICK THE BOTTOM OF YOUR TEACHER'S SHOE?

BE PRANKED WITH A FAKE RAT

OR

A FAKE SNAKE?

WOULD YOU RATHER...

EAT 3 WORMS

OR

LICK A BIRD POO STAINED PARK BENCH?

PROJECT THE SOUND OF YOUR FART 6 FEET AWAY BUT YOU'RE THE ONE THAT SMELLS

OR

THE SMELL OF YOUR FART 6 FEET AWAY AND YOU MAKE THE FARTING NOISE?

WOULD YOU RATHER...

EAT A ROTTEN BANANA

OR

EAT A CUP FULL OF GRASS?

EAT FRENCH FRIES THAT HAD
FALLEN INTO THE TOILET

OR

REMOVE A SOGGY BAND AID
FROM AN OLD MAN'S FOOT USING
ONLY YOUR TEETH?

WOULD YOU RATHER...

DRINK WITH YOUR NOSE

OR

PEE OUT OF YOUR EARS?

BE ABLE TO PROJECTILE VOMIT AT WILL

OR

SUMMON AN EARTH SHATTERING FART AT WILL?

WOULD YOU RATHER...

HAVE CHEWING GUM STUCK IN YOUR HAIR

OR

CHEWING GUM STUCK UP YOUR NOSTRILS?

HAVE ANTS CRAWLING THROUGH YOUR ARMPITS

OR

SUCK ON A STRANGER'S USED HANDKERCHIEF?

WOULD YOU RATHER...

HAVE WORMS COME OUT OF YOUR NOSE WHEN YOU SNEEZE

OR

BE POOPED ON BY A FLOCK OF PELICANS?

HAVE 3 TOES ON YOUR FACE INSTEAD OF A NOSE

OR

3 FINGERS ON EACH SIDE OF YOUR HEAD INSTEAD OF EARS?

WOULD YOU RATHER...

DRINK A FISH'S WEE WITH
A TEASPOON

OR

HAVE A 400 POUND SUMO
WRESTLER FART ON YOUR
HEAD?

POP YOUR FRIEND'S PIMPLE
AND LICK THE PUS

OR

YOUR FRIEND POP YOUR PIMPLE
AND LICK YOUR PUS?

WOULD YOU RATHER...

VOMIT ON YOUR GRANDPA

OR

HAVE YOUR GRANDPA VOMIT ON YOU?

USE BEAVER POOP AS BUILDING BLOCKS

OR

WEAR A STINKING, DEAD BEAVER AS A HAT?

WOULD YOU RATHER...

WATCH A MOVIE ABOUT THE HISTORY OF FARTS

OR

THE HISTORY OF POOP?

HAVE A BABY VOMIT ON YOUR FAVORITE SHIRT

OR

THROW UP YOUR FAVORITE MEAL ON A BABY?

WOULD YOU RATHER...

EAT A TEASPOON OF
OLD LADY BOOGERS

OR

A SMALL BOWL OF
DEAD FLIES?

WEAR A USED BABY DIAPER ON
YOUR HEAD AT SCHOOL

OR

GO TO SCHOOL WEARING A
GIANT DIAPER?

WOULD YOU RATHER...

EAT A BIG MAC YOU FOUND
IN A GARBAGE BIN

OR

A CHOCOLATE BAR YOU FOUND
IN A MUDDY PUDDLE?

EAT MASHED BANANA TOPPED
WITH A SPOONFUL OF SPIT

OR

A HOTDOG MADE WITH THE
SNOT OF 17 OLD MEN?

WOULD YOU RATHER...

FART NEXT TO YOUR GRANDMA

OR

YOUR GRANDMA FART
NEXT TO YOU?

FIND 5 POUNDS OF MOUSE POOP
IN YOUR REFRIGERATOR

OR

45 POUNDS OF HORSE POOP
IN YOUR CLOSET?

WOULD YOU RATHER...

HAVE A HUNDRED
COCKROACHES RUN OVER YOUR
LEGS

OR

A HUNDRED SPIDERS RUN OVER
YOUR ARMS?

ALL YOUR HAIR
FALL OUT

OR

ALL OF YOUR TEETH
FALL OUT?

WOULD YOU RATHER...

CONTROL THE SOUND OF YOUR FART SO IT SOUNDS LIKE A CAR HORN

OR

THE SMELL OF YOUR FART SO IT SMELLS LIKE GIRL'S PERFUME?

LICK CHEWING GUM OFF THE GROUND

OR

LICK A SKUNK?

WOULD YOU RATHER...

KISS A DEAD RAT

OR

EAT AN EARWIG?

HAVE MAGGOTS LIVING
IN YOUR HAIR

OR

HAVE WORMS LIVING IN YOUR
EARS AND NOSE?

WOULD YOU RATHER...

BRUSH YOUR TEETH WITH YOUR DIRTY FINGERS

OR

LET SOMEONE ELSE BRUSH YOUR TEETH WITH THEIR UNWASHED FINGERS?

DO THE BIGGEST FART EVER HEARD, BUT NO-ONE IS AROUND TO HEAR IT

OR

DO A BIG, SLOPPY, WET FART IN FRONT OF YOUR PARENTS AND THEIR FRIENDS?

WOULD YOU RATHER...

KISS A JELLYFISH

OR

LICK A ROTTEN FISH?

STEP IN DOG POOP WITH BARE FEET ONCE A DAY FOR THE REST OF YOUR LIFE

OR

STICK A STRAW INTO A TERMITE MOUND AND SUCK UP TERMITES FOR 20 SECONDS?

WOULD YOU RATHER...

HAVE A BABY PEE ON YOU

OR

THROW UP ON YOU?

WEAR THE SHIRT YOU'RE CURRENTLY WEARING FOR A MONTH

OR

THE UNDERWEAR THAT YOU'RE CURRENTLY WEARING FOR A WEEK?

WOULD YOU RATHER...

HAVE A RABBIT FART
ON YOU

OR

AN ELEPHANT FART ON YOU?

FLY A KITE MADE OF
DRIED BOOGERS

OR

PUT YOUR FINGER INSIDE A
ROTTING APPLE TO GIVE THE
WORM SOMETHING ELSE TO
NIBBLE ON?

WOULD YOU RATHER...

CLEAN YOUR ROOM WITH A BROOM MADE OF HUMAN HAIR

OR

WASH A CAR WITH YOUR OWN SPIT?

BURP AFTER EVERY KISS

OR

HAVE TO FART LOUDLY EVERY TIME YOU HAVE A SERIOUS CONVERSATION?

WOULD YOU RATHER...

GIVE UP ACCESS TO YOUR
COMPUTER AND SMARTPHONE

OR

HAVE AN OLD MAN'S EAR
FOR A NOSE?

HAVE THREE TEETH
PULLED OUT

OR

GROW THREE EXTRA TEETH ON
THE END OF YOUR TONGUE?

WOULD YOU RATHER...

EAT A LIVE ADULT SCORPION

OR

DRINK A TALL GLASS OF MUDDY WATER?

JUMP OUT OF A WINDOW AND TRY TO USE FARTS TO SLOW YOUR FALL

OR

JUMP OUT OF A WINDOW AND TRY TO LAND ON A ROTTING ELEPHANT?

WOULD YOU RATHER...

SNIFF A CAT'S BUTT

OR

SNIFF A DOG'S BUTT?

YOUR FRIEND'S BROTHER
BARFED ON YOUR BED

OR

A HAPPY, ELDERLY GENTLEMAN
DID A POOP ON YOUR PORCH?

WOULD YOU RATHER...

WAX AN OLD LADY'S
LEG HAIR

OR

PLUCK AN OLD MAN'S
EAR HAIR?

BE STUCK IN AN AQUARIUM
WITH A GREAT WHITE SHARK

OR

IN A ROOM WHERE THE FLOOR IS
COVERED BY 300 SPIDERS?

WOULD YOU RATHER...

FILL UP ALL YOUR FRIENDS' WATER BALLOONS WITH VOMIT WITHOUT TELLING THEM

OR

CHARGE THEM EXTRA FOR THE SERVICE?

HAVE A HAPPY, ELDERLY LADY SNEEZE IN YOUR FACE

OR

FART ON YOUR FACE?

WOULD YOU RATHER...

TOUCH YOUR FLOATING POOP

OR

TOUCH A DOG POOP IN THE PARK?

HAVE A BATH IN WARM VOMIT

OR

SLEEP UNDER A PILE OF USED BABY DIAPERS?

WOULD YOU RATHER...

FIND A COCKROACH HIDING IN YOUR CHEESEBURGER

OR

IN YOUR UNDERWEAR?

COOK PASTA IN A POT OF BOOGERS INSTEAD OF WATER

OR

COOK PASTA IN A POT OF SWEAT?

WOULD YOU RATHER...

EAT A LIVE GRASSHOPPER

OR

DRINK A GLASS OF BLENDED
FRIED ANTS?

HOLD A POISONOUS SNAKE
FOR AN HOUR

OR

A HUGE TARANTULA FOR
20 MINUTES?

WOULD YOU RATHER...

FART LOUDLY IN A QUIET LIBRARY

OR

BARF ON YOUR TEACHER'S SHOES?

RECEIVE A GIFT OF A JAR OF PICKLED EYEBALLS

OR

A GIFT-WRAPPED BOX OF DRIED ANIMAL POOPS?

WOULD YOU RATHER...

GO SWIMMING IN A
RIVER OF VOMIT

OR

DIVE INTO A POOL OF
ELEPHANT WEE?

DO ONE ABSOLUTELY
GIGANTIC FART ONCE A WEEK

OR

10 SMALL FARTS
EVERY DAY?

WOULD YOU RATHER...

HAVE A JOB PICKING UP LLAMA POOP

OR

ELEPHANT POOP?

USE A SMELLY SNAIL SHELL AS A SPOON TO EAT A BOWL OF SOUP

OR

HAVE A SMALL SNAIL CRAWL IN YOUR NOSE AND OUT YOUR MOUTH?

WOULD YOU RATHER...

EAT ANT FLAVORED
ICE CREAM

OR

DRINK ROTTEN WORM
FLAVORED SODA?

HAVE YOUR FARTS SOUND LIKE
A CAR BLASTING ITS HORN

OR

LIKE AN ANGRY LION
ROARING?

WOULD YOU RATHER...

WASH A PET WITH
YOUR TONGUE

OR

WASH YOUR DISHES WITH
YOUR TONGUE?

LICK THE SNOT OUT OF YOUR
BEST FRIEND'S NOSE

OR

LICK THE EARWAX OUT OF YOUR
BEST FRIEND'S EAR?

WOULD YOU RATHER...

FEED GRAPES TO A REAL AND VERY STINKY ZOMBIE

OR

FEED GRAPES TO AN ALLIGATOR BY HAND?

HOLD A SNAKE FOR 2 HOURS

OR

4 REALLY BIG SPIDERS FOR ONE HOUR?

WOULD YOU RATHER...

WEAR A JACKET MADE OF MOULDY SOCKS

OR

A HAT MADE FROM YOUR GRANDPA'S UNDERWEAR?

NEVER FART AGAIN BUT BURP CONSTANTLY

OR

NEVER BURP AGAIN BUT FART 6 TIMES A DAY?

WOULD YOU RATHER...

ONLY BE ABLE TO DRINK THE PUS FROM POPPED PIMPLES FOR A WEEK

OR

HAVE A BATH IN 10% ELEPHANT PEE?

EAT A ROTTEN APPLE

OR

LICK A SWEATY BODYBUILDER'S UNDERPANTS?

WOULD YOU RATHER...

EAT 16 LIVE
COCKROACHES

OR

EAT A BOOGER THE SIZE
OF A GUMBALL?

SUCK THE EYEBALL OUT OF
A DEAD FISH

OR

A DEAD RAT?

WOULD YOU RATHER...

HAVE CHEWING GUM STUCK
IN YOUR HAIR

OR

CHEWING GUM STUCK
UP YOUR NOSE?

ACCIDENTALLY FART REALLY
LOUDLY IN PUBLIC

OR

ACCIDENTALLY PEE YOURSELF
IN PUBLIC?

WOULD YOU RATHER...

FIND A POOP IN
THE BATHTUB

OR

FIND A POOP IN
THE SHOWER?

EAT A ROTTEN FISH AND
JELLY SANDWICH

OR

EAT A COCKROACH AND
CHOCOLATE SANDWICH?

WOULD YOU RATHER...

LOSE BOTH YOUR FEET

OR

BOTH YOUR HANDS?

HAVE 17 FRIED COCKROACHES FOR BREAKFAST EVERY MORNING

OR

HAVE TO SLEEP WITH 17 COCKROACHES CRAWLING ALL OVER YOU EVERY NIGHT?

WOULD YOU RATHER...

DRINK THE WATER OUT OF
A FISH TANK

OR

DRINK YOUR NEIGHBOR'S
TOILET WATER?

PERFORM A DANCE ROUTINE
WHILE FARTING THE WHOLE TIME

OR

RUN DOWN THE STREET
SHOUTING LOUDLY WEARING
A GIANT DIAPER?

WOULD YOU RATHER...

SLEEP IN A GARBAGE BIN
FOR A WEEK

OR

IN A PIGSTY FOR
2 NIGHTS?

USE YOUR FRIEND'S TOILET
WHEN YOU'VE GOT DIARRHEA

OR

HAVE A FRIEND WITH
DIARRHEA USE YOUR TOILET?

WOULD YOU RATHER...

HAVE PEPPER GET IN
YOUR EYES

OR

BREATHE PEPPER INTO
YOUR NOSE?

MARRY SOMEONE WHO IS
GORGEOUS BUT SMELLS
REALLY BAD

OR

MARRY SOMEONE WHO IS
UNATTRACTIVE BUT SMELLS
INCREDIBLY GOOD?

WOULD YOU RATHER...

BRUSH YOUR TEETH WITH FART FLAVORED TOOTHPASTE

OR

WASH YOUR HAIR WITH ROTTEN FISH GUTS?

EAT A CHUNK OF THE BUTT HAIR FROM A MONKEY

OR

HAVE A MONKEY NIBBLE ON YOUR LEFT FOOT?

WOULD YOU RATHER...

WASH YOUR HAIR WITH DIRTY DISHWATER

OR

BRUSH YOUR TEETH WITH A STRANGER'S SNOT?

SWIM TEN MILES THROUGH THE SEWER

OR

HAVE EVERY SONG YOU EVER HEAR FROM NOW ON BE MADE ENTIRELY OF FART SOUNDS?

WOULD YOU RATHER...

SNIFF A DOG'S BREATH

OR

A CAT'S BREATH?

EAT A WHOLE
POISON IVY PLANT

OR

A PIECE OF GUM YOU FOUND ON
THE UNDERSIDE OF
A PARK BENCH?

WOULD YOU RATHER...

HAVE LOTS OF LITTLE BABY SPIDERS COME OUT OF YOUR PIMPLE

OR

3 HUGE SPIDERS CRAWL ON YOUR HEAD?

DROP YOUR PHONE IN A 40 GALLON DRUM OF SNOT

OR

PERFORM SWEET TRICKS ON A SKATEBOARD WEARING A USED DIAPER AS A HELMET?

WOULD YOU RATHER...

PEE YOUR PANTS
WHEN YOU LAUGH

OR

PEE YOUR PANTS
WHEN YOU CRY?

HAVE A RAINBOW COLORED
CLOUD APPEAR WHEN YOU FART

OR

HAVE BURPS THAT SMELL
LIKE ROTTEN EGGS?

WOULD YOU RATHER...

EAT A FRIED MOUSE AND KETCHUP SANDWICH

OR

AN UNCOOKED DEAD BIRD AND CHILLI SAUCE SANDWICH?

LOOK THROUGH A TELESCOPE AND SEE THAT THE MOON IS JUST A GIANT ROUND POOP

OR

LOOK AT YOUR OWN CELLS UNDER A MICROSCOPE AND SEE THAT YOU ARE MADE UP OF BILLIONS OF TINY POOPS?

WOULD YOU RATHER...

POOP YOUR PANTS ON
A CROWDED BUS

OR

PEE YOUR PANTS ON
A ROLLERCOASTER?

WEAR YOUR DIRTY UNDERWEAR
ON YOUR HEAD AS A HAT

OR

YOUR DAD'S STINKY, GROSS
UNDERWEAR ON YOUR HEAD
AS A HAT WHEN YOU
MEET THE PRESIDENT?

WOULD YOU RATHER...

USE SAND PAPER TO
WIPE YOUR BUTT

OR

USE VINEGAR AS EYE DROPS?

HAVE 4 LARGE LIZARDS CRAWL
OVER YOU FOR 6 MINUTES

OR

6 BUCKETS OF MAGGOTS BE
DROPPED ON YOU FROM ABOVE?

WOULD YOU RATHER...

HAVE A HAPPY, ELDERLY GENTLEMAN FART ON YOUR HEAD

OR

WEAR A DIRTY DIAPER AS A HAT?

BE COVERED IN JELLO

OR

COVERED IN PEANUT BUTTER?

WOULD YOU RATHER...

LICK A BUSY
RESTROOM FLOOR

OR

A BUSY RESTROOM
DOOR HANDLE?

DRINK A SOGGY,
SQUISHED UP SLUG

OR

EAT A CRUNCHY,
BAKED COCKROACH?

WOULD YOU RATHER...

LICK YOUR FRIEND'S FOOT

OR

HAVE YOUR FRIEND LICK YOUR FOOT?

USE A ROTTING FISH AS A PILLOW

OR

SNIFF THE INSIDE OF A TOILET?

WOULD YOU RATHER...

BURP IN FRONT OF
YOUR TEACHER

OR

FART LOUDLY ON A
FIRST DATE?

EAT THE HOTTEST PEPPER
IN THE WORLD

OR

EAT ICE CREAM MADE
FROM DIRT?

WOULD YOU RATHER...

EAT A ROTTEN
EGG SALAD

OR

A VERY SMELLY
CHICKEN NUGGET?

SLEEP WITH A PILLOWCASE
FULL OF LIVE CREEPY CRAWLIES

OR

SLEEP ON A MATTRESS THAT
YOU KNOW IS MADE OF
DEAD INSECTS?

WOULD YOU RATHER...

EAT A RAW EGG

OR

LICK A MOUSE'S FOOT?

HAVE 20 SPIDERS CRAWL ON YOU FOR 20 MINUTES

OR

EAT A FRIED SPIDER SANDWICH?

WOULD YOU RATHER...

HAVE 2 HANDS AT THE END OF EACH ARM

OR

2 FEET AT THE END OF EACH LEG?

GET STUCK IN A BLUE WHALE'S BLOW HOLE

OR

HAVE TO BREATHE IN A BLUE WHALE'S FART?

WOULD YOU RATHER...

EAT A SMALL CAN OF
CAT FOOD

OR

4 ROTTEN APPLES
FULL OF WORMS?

LICK PUS FROM YOUR
FRIEND'S PIMPLE

OR

BE COVERED IN PUS FROM YOUR
FRIEND'S EXPLODING PIMPLES?

WOULD YOU RATHER...

KISS A FROG ON THE LIPS
FOR ONE MINUTE

OR

SWIM IN A SMELLY POND FULL
OF FLOATING ROTTEN FISH?

HAVE A MONKEY THROW
ITS POOP AT YOU

OR

HAVE A MONKEY SNEAK UP ON
YOU AND FART ON YOUR HEAD?

THANKS A BUNCH!

For reading our book!
We hope you have enjoyed these

WOULD YOU RATHER?
EWW! YUCK! GROSS!

scenarios as much as we did as we were
putting this book together.
If you could possibly leave a review of our
book we would really appreciate it. ☺

To see all our latest books or leave a review
just go to
RatherFunnyPress.com
Once again, thanks so much for reading!

PS. Don't forget to grab your free surprise gift
on the very next page!
Enjoy!
Thanks again! ☺

RatherFunnyPress.com

YOUR FREE SURPRISE GIFT!

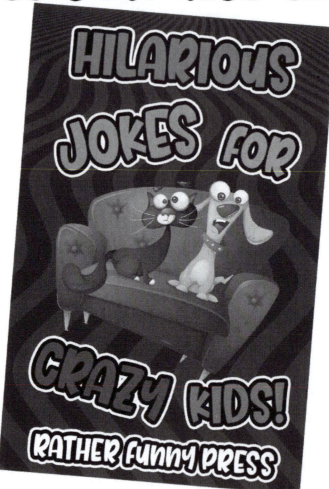

To grab your free copy of this brand new, hilarious Joke Book, just go to:

go.RatherFunnyPress.com

Enjoy!

RatherFunnyPress.com